THE CASE OF THE
GOBBLING
SQUASH

THE CASE OF THE GOBBLING SQUASH

by Elizabeth Levy
illustrated by Ellen Eagle

Simon and Schuster Books for Young Readers
Published by Simon & Schuster Inc.
New York

SIMON AND SCHUSTER
BOOKS FOR YOUNG READERS
Simon & Schuster Building
Rockefeller Center
1230 Avenue of the Americas
New York, New York 10020

10 9 8 7 6 5 4 3 2 1

10 9 8 7 6 5 4 3 2 1 (pbk.)

Library of Congress Cataloging-in-Publication Data
Levy, Elizabeth.   The case of the gobbling squash.
(A magic mystery)
SUMMARY: A young detective and her partner, an
amateur magician, solve a case involving missing bunnies,
a pink sock ghost, and a remote-control squash that
gobbles like a Thanksgiving turkey.
[1. Mystery and detective stories.   2. Magicians—
Fiction]   I. Eagle, Ellen, ill.   II. Title.
III. Series: Levy, Elizabeth. Magic mystery.
PZ7.L5827Cas 1988   [E]   88-4431
ISBN 0-671-63655-3

ISBN 0-671-68873-1 (pbk.)

Contents

1

No Job Too Small, Too Big, or Too Weird

The sign above Kate's booth in the Red Rock School gym read: MYSTERIES SOLVED: NO JOB TOO SMALL, TOO BIG, OR TOO WEIRD.

"You are the one who is weird, Kate," laughed Tracy. "Come on, I bet you haven't had a customer all day."

"Kate always has to be different," said Alex. "Since this is the Thanksgiving Fair, I'm surprised she's not selling Easter bunnies."

"Ms. Sugarman said to come up with something original this year," said Kate. "I thought a detective booth would do great business, but so far I haven't raised a cent." Kate had read hundreds of mysteries; but in books, detectives, even kid detectives, got business right away.

"Our booth has so many customers that Mr. Mullen wants a wet suit," said Tracy. She and Jennifer were running the Dunk the Principal booth at the school fair.

"Are you sure you guys don't have a problem I can help with?" asked Kate.

"I don't know how I'm going to learn my lines for the Thanksgiving pageant," said Jennifer. "Princess Squashblossom has such a big part."

Alex groaned and winked at Kate. Ever since Jennifer had won the leading role in the Thanksgiving pageant, she had talked of nothing else.

"Uh, excuse me," a voice said. Max stood at the back of the group. "I've got a problem," he said. He worked his way up to the front. "It's confidential," he whispered to Kate.

Kate got out her notebook. "Excuse me, guys. I've finally got a client. You'll have to give us a little privacy."

"Max must have a pretty weird problem if he's coming to you," teased Alex. Max blushed.

"Alex has a motor mouth, but he never means anything too nasty by it," Kate said to Max. "Now get lost, you guys. A private detective needs privacy."

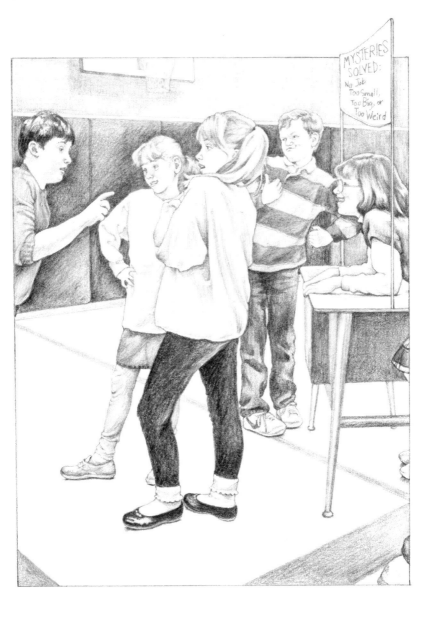

"What's the problem?" Kate asked after the other kids took off. Kate didn't know much about Max. He was just one of those in-between kids. He was smart, but not the smartest in the class; good at sports, but not the greatest.

"My bunny is missing," said Max. "She's been missing a whole week."

"Not an Easter bunny joke," exclaimed Kate. "Did Alex send you?"

"This isn't a joke," Max said. "I have a real problem. I have to find my bunny or my mom will kill me. Besides, he was slow."

"Why do you want a slow bunny?" asked Kate.

"It's a secret," said Max.

"You can't keep secrets from me," Kate argued. "I'm your detective. You're supposed to tell me everything."

"Promise not to make fun of me?"

"Why would I do that?"

"Because you always make jokes," said Max. "Maybe that's why you're so popular. I can't tell jokes."

Kate did like to tell jokes, but she never thought of herself as someone who made fun of other people. Maybe Alex was like that, but not her. "I promise not to make fun of you," she said.

"I practice magic," whispered Max. "I don't want anyone to know."

"Why not?" asked Kate.

"I don't want to talk about it," said Max.

"You're weird."

Max pointed to Kate's private detective sign. "You said 'No job too weird.'"

"You're right," said Kate. "I like weird cases. This is going to be fun." Finally she had a case with secrets, missing bunnies, even magic. Things were looking up.

2

The Runaway Ace of Diamonds

After the school fair Kate rode her bicycle to Max's house. "I'm a detective, ma'am," said Kate when Max's mother answered the door. "I'm here to see Max."

"Go on up," Max's mother said with a smile.

Max was in his room shuffling a deck of cards. His desk was littered with cards, scarves, plastic cups, and egg-shaped Ping-Pong balls. A big, floppy-eared rabbit sat in a cage on the window sill.

"Oh, no," said Kate. "You found him already."

"No," said Max, not even looking up. "That's Zippo. He's the fast one."

"The only thing moving is his nose," said Kate. She wiggled her nose back.

"As long as you're here, I've got another mystery for you to solve," said Max.

"Great! What's that?" asked Kate eagerly.

Max held up three aces: the Ace of Clubs, Spades, and Diamonds. "It's the Case of the Runaway Ace," he said. He handed the cards to Kate. "You shuffle the deck," he said. "Maybe the ace won't run away from you."

Kate shuffled. She even made a bridge.

"Now find the Ace of Diamonds," said Max.

Kate went through the deck, but she couldn't find it.

"I told you it keeps running away," said Max. "It must like you." Max reached into Kate's pocket and pulled out the Ace of Diamonds.

"How did you do that?" asked Kate.

"Magic," said Max, smiling.

"You're really good. I wish I could do something like that."

"I wish you could find my bunny," said Max. "That's why I hired you, remember."

"Right," said Kate. She took out her notebook. "Did anything suspicious happen the day your bunny disappeared?"

"No, but Fast Eddie was a little slower than usual."

"You named a slow bunny Fast Eddie?" asked Kate.

"He wasn't so slow when I bought him."

"Can you show me how you used the bunny? Maybe it will give me some clues."

Max blushed. "I pull him out of a hat," he said.

"Wonderful!" exclaimed Kate. "Do it with Zippo there."

"I don't show anybody my tricks," said Max. "I just do them in my room."

"But that's silly," said Kate. "I bet half the fun is doing it on stage."

Max shook his head. "Not for me. I get all sweaty and embarrassed."

"You can do the trick for me," said Kate. "I'm a private detective. So this is like a private show."

"Okay," said Max. "But for this trick, I need time to prepare. Get into the closet."

Kate got into the closet. Max shut the door behind her. "Hey, it stinks in here," Kate shouted.

"You're the one who wanted me to do this trick," Max shouted back through the closet door. Kate held her nose.

"How long have your socks been in here?" Kate yelled.

"Just be quiet," said Max. "You asked for a very tough trick."

"How about a simpler one—like making this smell disappear," shouted Kate.

When Max let Kate out of the closet, he was wearing what looked like his father's old tuxedo coat.

"Notice that my hands are empty." Max waved his hands in the air, but the tuxedo jacket flopped down over his wrists.

Max tossed a black top hat to Kate. She caught it like a frisbee. It was empty. She turned it upside down and put it up to her mouth. "I'm talking through my hat," she said.

"Is that supposed to be funny?" Max asked.

Kate sighed and handed him back the hat. Max held it upside down. "You agree that it is empty?"

Kate nodded.

Max reached inside the hat and pulled out a silk scarf. He pulled out another scarf and then another and another. "Ta ta!" he shouted.

Kate clapped.

Max pointed to the inside of the hat. "No bunny."

Then he reached inside the hat and brought out Zippo.

"Amazing!" cried Kate. "How did you do it?"

"A magician never tells his secret," said Max.
"It's part of our code."

Kate patted Zippo and wrinkled her nose.

"I think you might be violating some kind of health code," said Kate. "He smells."

Suddenly Kate was smiling. "Listen," she said. "I'll make a deal with you. I'll find the missing bunny, and you don't have to pay me. I was going to ask for a dollar up front."

"What's the catch?"

"If I find your bunny, you and I go into business together."

"What business?"

"The magic business. I can class up your act."

"I thought you were a detective."

Kate sighed. "The detective business isn't all that it's cracked up to be. At the Thanksgiving Fair you were my only customer. But I have a nose for crime. Let's make a bet. I find your bunny, and you let me help you take your act in front of the class."

"I'm not sure," said Max.

"What do you have to lose?" asked Kate. "You've already lost a bunny. Give me a chance."

"Okay, okay," said Max. "But only if you find my bunny."

"Stand back," said Kate, opening the closet door.

3

The Funny Bunny Business

Kate took a magic wand and poked a pile of clothes in the back corner of the closet floor.

"Uh-oh," said Kate.

"What's wrong now?" asked Max, trying to peer over her shoulder.

"Do you want the good news or the bad news first?" asked Kate.

"The good news."

"I found your bunny."

"That's great. What's the bad news?"

"She's busy," said Kate. "Fast Eddie should be called Fast Edwina."

"What do you mean *she*?" Max asked. "And how can a bunny be busy?"

"Bunnies can be busy," said Kate. "Especially mommy bunnies."

Kate stepped aside and let Max look into the closet. Edwina Bunny lay on her side. Nestled next to her were four baby bunnies.

"Aren't they cute?" exclaimed Kate.

"This is a disaster," said Max. "My mom will never let me keep them."

"If this was Easter we could sell the bunnies," said Kate. "Too bad you can't wave a magic wand and turn them into turkeys."

Max groaned.

Just then there was a knock on the door. "Who is it?" Max asked.

"It's Mom, honey," said Max's mother. "I brought you up a snack."

"Uhh, we don't need one," stammered Max. But Kate had already opened the door.

Max's mother almost dropped the milk and cookies when she saw the litter of bunnies.

"It's not my fault," said Max. "I asked for two males." Max's mother frowned at the bunnies. "I told you these bunnies were not a good idea. Your magic is getting out of hand."

"Maybe Kate wants one?" asked Max hopefully.

"We've got a dog," said Kate. "A very big dog...."

"You absolutely cannot keep them," said Max's mother. "You'll have to find someone who will take those bunnies before Thanksgiving, or you won't buy any new magic tricks for a year. I mean it, Max. I'll take away all your catalogs."

"How am I going to find anyone who will take a bunny three weeks before Thanksgiving?" wailed Max.

"Don't worry," said Kate. "I'll help." She took the milk and cookies from Max's mother and half pushed her out the door.

Max groaned. "You've helped too much already. It's been one disaster after another since I hired you."

"We could hold a bunny auction at the Thanksgiving pageant," Kate suggested.

Max shook his head. "Not too many people want bunnies," he said, "even at Easter."

Max went to a shelf and consulted a big book. "There's a trick called Metamorphosis. Houdini did it when he was a boy. It means changing one thing into another. I could change bunnies into turkeys."

"A perfect Thanksgiving trick," said Kate.

"But I need an assistant to do the trick."

"Me," shouted Kate.

Max closed the book. "Even if we could do the trick, we'd still be stuck with the bunnies. The audience thinks they've disappeared, but they're just hidden."

"If we got our act into the pageant, we could give a bunny away to each class. It could be our finale."

"The pageant's all set," said Max. "Ms. Sugarman handed out all the roles."

"I can talk Ms. Sugarman into putting in our act," said Kate. "Trust me."

"We don't even know if we can do the trick," Max argued.

"Sure we can. We'll practice. We've got a few weeks. And you're great. You just need a few jokes."

"I don't feel ready to perform in public," said Max.

"With me at your side, you'll be fine," said Kate. "Besides, how else are you going to get rid of those bunnies?"

"It would be a neat trick to try," Max admitted. "And a lot of magic is easier if you have an assistant."

"Partner," corrected Kate. "We're partners. We're in the funny bunny business together until we unload these rabbits. Then who knows where our partnership will take us...."

4

It's the Thanksgiving Bunny!

On Monday Kate rushed into class to talk to Ms. Sugarman before the bell rang. "Me and Max have got to be in the Thanksgiving pageant," said Kate.

"Max and I," corrected Ms. Sugarman. "Besides, you are both in the chorus already. You are an Indian and Max is a Pilgrim."

"No, no, we've got to have bigger roles," said Kate. "Max and I have got the greatest addition to the show."

"Ms. Sugarman," said Jennifer. "I spent all weekend memorizing my Princess Squashblossom lines."

"My uncle's a barber," said Alex. "And he's lending me a bunch of toupees for scalps."

"The Indians at the first Thanksgiving were friendly," said Kate. "They wouldn't carry scalps."

Ms. Sugarman sighed. "Kate, it's really too late to change things now. All the roles have been assigned."

"Why do you want a bigger part?" Tracy asked Kate.

"Not for me," said Kate. "For Max."

"Max!" exclaimed Tracy. "Max never opens his mouth."

Max slipped into the room and quietly sat at his desk.

The bell rang. Monday morning was the free writing period in class. Kate sat down and started writing as fast as she could. Her hand hurt by the time she finished. When Ms. Sugarman asked if anyone wanted to read aloud, Kate waved her hand in the air. So did Jennifer.

"Please, please," begged Kate until Ms. Sugarman called on her.

"Kate probably just wrote something silly," said Jennifer.

Kate was famous for never writing anything serious. "I did not," protested Kate. "This is very moving."

Ms. Sugarman coughed. "Kate, why don't you read it to us. We're the ones who are supposed to be moved."

"The title is 'The Magical Thanksgiving Bunny,'" Kate began. "Once there was a bunny that wanted to be invited to Thanksgiving. The Thanksgiving Bunny had heard that the Pilgrims always invited turkeys to a great feast. The bunny had got it mixed up. He didn't know that the turkeys got eaten."

"What's the bunny's name?" asked Alex.

"Max," said Kate.

Max turned several shades of red.

"Max was a master bunny magician," said Kate.

"I don't think Kate wrote all this down," said Jennifer. "We're supposed to write it all down, aren't we, Ms. Sugarman?"

Alex snapped his teeth at Max. "I want to hear the part where this bunny gets skinned and eaten."

Kate continued. "Bunny Max needed a partner, so he talked his friend Kate into helping him. She was a very smart bunny."

Max put his head down on the desk.

"When they got to the edge of the forest, Max

made Kate put on a turkey costume. The Pilgrims were very thankful. 'Look,' one of them said. 'A turkey is marching right into our pot.'

"'What pot?' asked Bunny Kate. 'I'm here for the feast.'

"'Indeed you are,' said Princess Squashblossom." Kate glanced at Jennifer.

Kate continued. "Princess Squashblossom grabbed Kate and popped her right into the pot.

"'HELP! MAX! HELP!' shouted Bunny Kate.

"Max jumped out of the woods. He waved his magic wand over the pot, and Kate jumped out of her turkey costume, and...and...and I guess that's the end of my story," said Kate.

"It's not a very good ending," said Alex.

"Yeah, it's not magical," said Tracy. "You said the title was 'The Magical Thanksgiving Bunny,' but there wasn't much magic."

Max had taken his head off his desk to listen to the kids criticize Kate's story.

Now he stood up. "The bunny called Max was very embarrassed, but he didn't want his friend Kate to be eaten," said Max. "He decided to teach Princess Squashblossom and the Pilgrims that the animals of the forest were smart. He told Bunny Kate to hop like a bunny and bring him a glass of water."

22

The whole class laughed. Max liked the sound.

Kate hopped over to the classroom sink and put some water in a glass. She handed the glass to Max.

"Now I need a coin," said Max. "Do any of you Pilgrims have a coin?"

"I've got one," said Alex. "Just try to make it disappear, Mr. Funny Bunny."

Max held out a handkerchief. "Will you please put the coin in the handkerchief?" he said to Alex.

Max put the handkerchief over the glass and dropped the coin into the glass. Everyone could hear the *clink* as the coin dropped.

Max lifted the handkerchief. The coin was in the bottom of the glass. "Oh, dear," said Max. "It didn't work. The coin's still there."

"I knew it wouldn't work," said Alex.

Max covered the glass with the handkerchief and put a rubber band around the handkerchief to make it airtight.

"Blow on it, Alex," Max said. "It needs some garlic breath."

Then Max took the rubber band off the glass and lifted the handkerchief. The coin was gone!

"How did you do that?" Alex demanded.

"Trade secret," said Max.

"Ms. Sugarman," said Kate. "Don't you think Max's magic act belongs in the Thanksgiving pageant?"

"Well," said Ms. Sugarman. "Magic is always fun, but you'd only have a few weeks to practice."

"Perfect timing," said Kate. "By then the bunnies will be ready to leave home."

"What's that?" asked Ms. Sugarman.

"Uh....It's just something magicians say."

Max crossed his eyes.

"We can be ready," said Kate. "We can do an even more spectacular trick. You won't believe your eyes!"

The class voted to put Kate and Max's magic act into the Thanksgiving pageant.

As they were leaving school that day, Max looked nervous. Kate grinned. "I told you if you stuck with me we'd go far," she said.

"Yeah," said Max. "That's why I'm worried. What if we go too far?"

5

Gobbles and Gurbs

Every day after school, Kate and Max went straight to Max's house to practice their magic act. In order to do the spectacular Metamorphosis, Kate first had to climb into a big bag.

"Make gobbling noises!" Max ordered. But no matter how hard she tried Kate's gobbles sounded like goose honks.

Finally Max let Kate out of the bag. "We're going to be a flop," he said. "The whole trick depends on your fooling the audience with gobbles."

"I didn't know perfect gobbles were part of the job," complained Kate. Then she jumped up. "Don't worry. Tomorrow afternoon I'll have the perfect gobble. Just you wait."

The next day Kate went back to Max's house after school.

As soon as Kate got back into the bag, the sweetest, truest gobble sounds came out.

Max opened the bag and helped Kate out. "How did you do that?"

"I fooled the magician," Kate grinned. "It's my Turkey Yelper." She showed Max a small wooden box with a stick on a spring. When Kate pushed the stick with her finger, the box talked turkey.

"My uncle lives in the country, and he came in third once in a contest for the best turkey caller," Kate explained. "He also gave me a tape of turkey calls."

Max had a cassette recorder in his room. Kate put in the tape and the room filled up with gobbles and gurbs and clucks.

"This is terrific!" exclaimed Max. "Now the trick is going to be better than ever."

"We'd better practice again," said Kate. "I want to get it just right."

By the day of the pageant, Kate and Max had practiced their trick so many times they were sure it would go perfectly.

Before school began, Kate and Max brought Edwina, Zippo, and the little bunnies to the prop room and left them in their cage.

The pageant was at two o'clock in the afternoon, and all the parents were invited. By lunch time Max was a bundle of nerves.

Finally it was time to put on their costumes.

"I wish I didn't look so silly," said Kate, putting on her bunny ears and a skirt of turkey feathers. Jennifer looked beautiful in her Princess Squashblossom costume made out of real suede with beading all down the front.

"It was you who got us into this," hissed Max. He was wearing bunny ears sticking out of a black top hat. "Do you want to practice the trick one last time?" he asked.

"If I do Metamorphosis again, I'll turn into a real bunny myself."

"We have to be very careful about getting the bunnies into the sack," warned Max.

"No problem," said Kate. "The bunnies are all in a cage in the sack already."

"I want to check them," said Max. "A magician always checks everything before the show."

"Oh, all right," said Kate. "But we already put the cage of bunnies in the sack this morning. Come on."

Kate waddled onto the stage in her costume.

The curtain was closed. On the other side of the curtain, she could hear the little kids marching in. The pageant would start in less than fifteen minutes.

Kate went to the prop room where she had left the cage. The sack lay empty on the floor.

"Max!" Kate screamed. "They're gone. All the bunnies are missing!"

"Oh, no," groaned Max, staring at the empty sack. "We can't do the act without those bunnies."

Kate beamed. "It's a real mystery. The Case of the Disappearing Turkey Bunnies. Finally I have a case."

"It's not a mystery, Kate," said Max, "it's a disaster."

6

The Pink Sock Ghost

Kate picked up the sack and turned it inside out. "Ah, ha! A turkey feather! It's a clue! With this turkey feather, I can open doors. Get it? A tur-key to unlock the mystery!"

"You're the one who's covered in turkey feathers," said Max. "It probably came from your costume."

"Mine are real turkey feathers," said Kate. "Straight from Uncle Billy. This is plastic."

Alex walked by wearing a plastic headdress.

Kate ran up to him and stood on tiptoes.

"What are you doing?" Alex demanded. Kate studied the headdress. None of the feathers matched.

"Uh, nothing," said Kate.

"Was it Alex?" Max demanded.

"I don't think so," said Kate.

"Maybe someone did us a favor," said Max. "We needed to get rid of the bunnies anyhow."

"But not like this!" cried Kate. "We don't know if they've found a good home. Besides, it ruins our act. This was our big chance to show our stuff."

"I'm not sure we were ready anyhow," said Max. "We can tell Ms. Sugarman that we can't go on."

"The show always goes on," said Kate. "That must be in the magician's code." Kate put her finger on her nose. "Don't worry, Max. I've got a nose for crime. I've got a plan to catch the bunny snatcher. Can you do a trick that will scare the kids out of the dressing room? We need to search it."

"I've got my flying head," said Max, bringing out a pink sock from his magic kit. He took off his shoe and put it on. "This will scare everyone out of the dressing room in three seconds."

"Your socks?" said Kate. "That's smelly, but not scary."

"Come with me," said Max. He hopped behind a side curtain. "Close it so that there's no light."

Kate pulled the curtain around them. A ghostly pink face flew near her nose. Kate yelped.

"Shh," said Max, opening the curtain. "It's just my sock. I painted a face in dayglo paint on it. In the dark, when I lie on my back and wave it in the air, it looks just like a ghost."

"Perfect," said Kate. She whispered her plan to Max.

Kate and Max went backstage where everyone had gathered. Tracy was tilting her Pilgrim's hat at a rakish angle. Jennifer took one last look at herself in the mirror. Then she fussed with her big basket full of squash.

Kate signaled to Max. Suddenly all the backstage lights went out.

"Oh, no," said Ms. Sugarman. "Not a blackout right before we're supposed to go on."

"A ghost!" screamed Jennifer as a pink face floated in the darkness.

All the kids ran like bunnies into the hall, all except Kate and Max.

Max handed Kate the flashlight from his magic kit.

Kate beamed the light around the room. "I know those bunnies are here somewhere," she said. "It smells just like the bottom of your closet."

Kate picked up Tracy's hat, expecting to see bunnies hopping out. Nothing.

"This is hopeless!" exclaimed Max.

Kate wrinkled her nose. "It's close! It's close!" she said.

Max sat down next to Jennifer's basket. Suddenly he wrinkled his nose, too.

"Kate, Kate! Here!" he cried.

Kate and Max pulled the vegetables out from the top of the basket. The bunnies were in their cage at the bottom of the basket, happily munching a carrot.

"Jennifer did it!" said Kate. "She didn't want our act in the pageant. Princess Squashblossom took our bunnies. I'd like to squash her."

Max rummaged around in his magic kit. "Remember that tape of turkey gobbles you had?" said Max. "I packed it just in case the Turkey Yelper broke."

"I wish Jennifer were a turkey so I could wring her neck."

"I know how we can do our trick on stage and teach Jennifer a lesson," said Max with a smile on his face.

Max told Kate his plan. Kate grinned back. "Max, you're just the kind of partner I always wanted," she said.

7

The Gobbling Squash

The lights dimmed. The spotlight hit the curtain. Ms. Sugarman put her hand on Kate's shoulder. "Ready for the finale?" she whispered.

Kate nodded, her mouth dry. Then she stepped through the curtain onto center stage. "Hi," she said. "I'm the Thanksgiving bunny, and I've got a story for you! I was a silly bunny. I lived in the forest, and I heard that the Pilgrims, the new guys in town, had the turkeys for Thanksgiving. I thought I was being left out of a great party, so I disguised myself as a turkey and went to the celebration. Come along with me."

The curtain opened on the Indians and the Pilgrims at the Thanksgiving feast, all gathered around a big pot.

"Ah, ha! A turkey's walked right into our pot," said Tracy, the head Pilgrim. "We have much to be thankful for."

"Yum, yum," said Princess Squashblossom. "A big plump turkey for the eating." That line hadn't been in the script.

The audience laughed. Kate glared at Jennifer through her turkey costume.

"No! No!" cried Kate. "I'm not a turkey. I'm a bunny!"

"She's lying," said Tracy.

Suddenly Max the Magic Bunny stepped onto the stage.

"Wait a minute, you Pilgrims and Indians," said Max. "You're not cooking the turkey the right way. You need to put it in a sack to seal in the flavor."

Jennifer and Tracy put Kate in a sack and covered her up.

"We have to make sure she doesn't get out," said Max. "We need a volunteer from each class to come up and lock her in."

A child from each grade came up on stage. Max helped a little first grader put a lock on the sack.

Max and all the kids lowered Kate into the pot, sack and all. "She went in a turkey, but she'll come out a bunny. Can you hear her gobbles?" he asked the first grader.

The first grader put his ear to the sack. "I don't hear anything."

Suddenly loud gobbling noises came out of Jennifer's basket. The gobbling got louder and louder.

Jennifer put her hands over the basket as if trying to drown out the noise.

"What do we have here?" asked Max. "Turkey in the basket?"

Princess Squashblossom turned very pink. "I don't know why my basket is making that disgusting noise!" Jennifer wailed.

"Perhaps the Princess is a turkey?" suggested Max. He went over to Jennifer's basket. He pulled out a giant squash that was gobbling like a turkey. Max held the gobbling squash up to his ear. He shook it. He held it high in the air so everyone could get a good look at the gobbling squash.

The audience could not stop laughing.

"Let's see what happened to the turkey in the pot," said Max.

He went over to the pot and pulled the sack from the pot.

"Will you help me see what's in here?" he said to the volunteers.

Inside the sack were Max's bunnies.

"But where's Kate?" asked Max.

He tossed the gobbling squash at Jennifer.

"What have you done with my assistant, Princess Squashblossom?" Max demanded.

"Partner!" cried Kate, jumping out of Jennifer's basket.

The audience applauded and applauded.

Jennifer turned red as a tomato.

"That'll teach you to try to play a trick on a magician," said Kate. "You took the bunnies to spoil our act. But you just made our trick even better."

"I'm sorry," said Jennifer. "Just stop my squash from gobbling. Please."

Kate took the squash from Jennifer and pressed the button on the remote control device. Kate and Max had hidden the cassette of turkey calls in Jennifer's squash. The squash stopped gobbling.

Kate held up her hand to stop the applause. "As a special Thanksgiving prize, each class is going to get a bunny!" she said. Kate handed each of the volunteers a bunny. "How's that for Thanksgiving magic!"

Ms. Sugarman pulled the curtain down. "You

were great," she said to Kate and Max. The other kids gathered around and shook Max's hand. "That was some magic," said Alex.

"Thanks," said Max. "I couldn't have done it without Kate."

Jennifer took off her headdress. "I'm sorry," she said. "It was stupid of me."

"Never fool with a detective like Kate," said Max.

"That's what she said about a magician like you," said Jennifer as she went off to get out of her costume.

Max started to pack up his magic tricks. He looked around for Kate. She had taken off her turkey feathers.

Max held out his hand. "Shake, partner," he said.

"I told you we'd be terrific," said Kate. "And we got homes for all the bunnies."

"I kept one," said Max.

"Which one?" asked Kate.

"Edwina."

"Oh, no," said Kate. "Knowing Edwina, we'll be in the funny bunny business for a long time."

"Why not?" asked Max. "We've got a great act."

8

How to do Max's Magic Tricks

Runaway Ace

WHAT YOU NEED:

a deck of cards

BEFOREHAND:

Put the Ace of Diamonds in your pocket. Hold the other three aces in your hand so that the Ace of Hearts looks like the Ace of Diamonds. (See illustration.)

WHAT THE AUDIENCE SEES:

The audience sees three aces. One of them looks like the Ace of Diamonds. Then you put

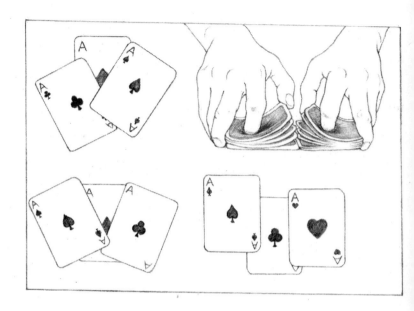

the aces into the deck and let someone in the audience shuffle. He or she won't be able to find the Ace of Diamonds.

SECRET:

The real Ace of Diamonds is in your pocket. While the person in the audience is shuffling the deck, you hide the real Ace of Diamonds in the palm of your hand and then pretend to pull it from the person's pocket.

Pulling a Rabbit Out of an Empty Hat

This trick should be done with a toy rabbit.

WHAT YOU NEED:

    a top hat
    a toy bunny
    a roll of scarves tied together
    a black bag with a drawstring

BEFOREHAND:

Put the bunny in the black bag and hang it over a chair. Hide the scarves up your sleeve.

WHAT THE AUDIENCE SEES:

The audience can examine the empty hat. You pull out a roll of scarves from the seemingly empty hat. You pile the scarves on the chair. Then you pull a bunny out of the hat.

SECRET:

The scarves that you have hidden up your sleeve keep the audience's attention while you put the bag into the hat.

When you show the top hat with your left hand, you put the scarves in your right hand which is hidden behind the brim of the hat. Then you reach into the hat with your right hand and drop the scarves into the hat.

As you pull out the scarves, your audience will watch as you drop each one. As you pull out the last one, raise your left hand high in the air and say "Ta ta!" The audience will follow your left hand and not notice that with your right hand you have put the black bag with the bunny into the hat. You pull the bunny out of the black bag which remains hidden in the hat.

The Coin Disappears into a Glass of Water

WHAT YOU NEED:

a coin (a half dollar is best)
an ordinary glass
a handkerchief or napkin
a rubber band

BEFOREHAND:

Have the rubber band in your pocket.

WHAT THE AUDIENCE SEES:

Someone from the audience can put the coin in the cloth. You cover the glass with the handkerchief. Everyone can hear the coin hit the glass. When you lift the handkerchief, you show the audience that the coin is definitely in the water. Then you cover the glass again, making sure the handkerchief is held tight by the rubber band. When you lift the handkerchief, the coin has disappeared.

SECRET:

The coin is in the palm of your hand, not in the glass. The coin hits the side of the glass and falls into your fingers. The audience can see the coin because the water makes it look like it is at the bottom of the glass, which is resting on your palm.

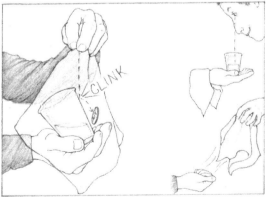

When you reach into your pocket for the rubber band, do it with the hand holding the coin. Drop the coin into your pocket and pull out the rubber band.

When the handkerchief is lifted, the glass is empty.

Metamorphosis

WHAT YOU NEED:

a trick chain from a magic store
a sack
a large stage prop pot or a screen to put around the sack
a cassette recorder (with a remote control device, if possible)
a cassette of animal noises
a dried squash or other vegetable, cut open so that you can put in the cassette

WHAT THE AUDIENCE SEES:

The audience saw Kate locked inside a sack. But the chain was a trick one, and as soon as she was put into the sack, Kate was out of the chains.

As soon as she was put into the pot, she got out of the sack. There were two sacks with identical locks. The bunnies were already in the bottom of the pot in the other sack. While Max was holding up the gobbling squash, Kate slipped backstage, ran around to the other side, and got into the basket.

THE SECRET:

The secret is the magician's greatest trick: misdirection. Everyone was looking and listening to the gobbling squash, which was activated by a remote control device in Max's pocket. (If you have no remote control device, leave a long blank space on your tape.) No one paid any attention to the pot. Kate had to move quickly. The trick depended on split-second timing, and on Max's hold on the audience's attention. Kate was ready to get out of the pot when Max took the gobbling squash from Jennifer's basket. A screen was around the pot. Kate hopped out of the pot and ran backstage before anyone could see her.

Max held the audience's attention and that's why he turned out to be a great magician.